The Lazy Bear

For Clare and Rebecca
(WHO MADE THE GRASS GROW)

First published 1973 by Oxford University Press, London, England
First American publication 1974 by Franklin Watts, Inc.
Copyright © 1973 by Brian Wildsmith
Library of Congress Catalog Card Number: 73-8398
SBN: 531-01559-9
Printed in U.S.A.

The Lazy Bear

BRIAN WILDSMITH

FRANKLIN WATTS, INC. NEW YORK, N.Y. 1974

Once upon a time, there was a bear who was so kind and thoughtful that all his neighbors were his friends.

The bear liked to go for long walks, and one day, at the top of a hill, he found a wagon. It had been left there by the woodcutter.

The bear had never seen a wagon before, and he walked
all round it, and sniffed it, and at last sat in it.

To his surprise the wagon began to move.
As it rolled downhill, the bear felt rather
frightened. But, by the time it reached the
bottom, he was enjoying the ride.

He liked it so much that he pushed the wagon right back up the hill, and rode down again. Time after time he pushed the wagon up the hill and rode down at great speed.

"This is fun," he thought. "But I don't like having to push the wagon up the hill much."

Every day he rode the wagon from morning till night, but the more he enjoyed the rides, the more he hated the hard work of pushing the wagon uphill.

Then he had an idea. He went to look for his friend the racoon. He told him all about the wagon, and the wonderful rides, and invited the racoon to come and see for himself.

The racoon was naturally curious, so he went along with the bear.

On the way, they met the deer.
"Come with us," said the bear, "and have a ride in my wagon."
The deer was naturally curious, so he went along with the bear and the racoon.

7

On the way, they met the goat.
"Come with us," said the bear, "and have a ride in my wagon."
The goat was naturally curious, so he went along with the bear, the racoon and the deer.

In a very short time they were all
riding down the hill at a wonderful
speed.
"This is lovely," said the racoon.
"This is marvelous," said the deer.
"Great, just great!" said the goat.

At the bottom, they all got out – except the bear, who sat tight.

"Hey! Come and help push," cried the racoon, the deer and the goat.

"What, me?" said the bear. "If I let you ride in my wagon, the least you can do is to push me back up the hill, don't you think?"

And he looked so fierce, that his friends were too frightened to argue.

So they all went on riding downhill, and the racoon, the deer and the goat went on pushing the bear back to the top. "What shall we do?" they whispered to each other. "This is very tiring, but if we give up, the bear will get us. He's not his usual kind self at all."

Then, when they were pushing the bear uphill for the hundredth time, the goat had an idea.

"Listen," he whispered, urgently. "I know what we'll do." The others bent their heads towards him and listened to his plan.

The bear was busy enjoying the scenery and noticed nothing – until they reached the top of the hill. Then – "Right!" shouted the goat. "Over the top with him." And the wagon, with the bear in it, went hurtling down the other side of the hill.

Faster and faster sped the wagon, until it crashed at the bottom. The bear was flung out, head over heels, and landed right side up in a shallow pond.

But, worst of all, when he looked round, he saw all the other animals of the forest standing on the bank, and laughing at him. "It serves you right," they said. "It was very unkind of you to bully your friends like that."
But they helped him out of the pond, and set the wagon upright for him.

"Now you must push the racoon, the deer and the goat uphill," they said. "Then you will know how they felt having to push a great, heavy animal like you."
So the bear pushed his friends up the hill, not once, but many times, and each time he understood a little more how badly he had behaved.

At last, he said, "I am truly sorry for what I did, and I won't do it ever again." At that, the racoon, the deer and the goat invited the bear to climb into the wagon, and they all rode downhill at a glorious pace. And at the bottom, they all got out and pushed the wagon back again, together.